SO WHAT?

Story by Miriam Cohen

Pictures

A Young Yearling Book

Published by
Dell Publishing
a division of
The Bantam Doubleday Dell Publishing Group, Inc.
1 Dag Hammarskjold Plaza
New York, New York 10017

Yearling ® TM 913705, Dell Publishing Co., Inc.

ISBN: 0-440-40048-1

Reprinted by arrangement with William Morrow and Company, Inc. on behalf
of Greenwillow Books

Printed in the United States of America

April 1988

10 9 8 7 6 5 4 3 2 1

W

For William and Sara Hull,
two wonderful teachers
who taught me about "hard" and "easy"

First grade was having recess.
Jim and Paul and Danny and Sara
were hanging upside down
on the jungle gym.

Paul and Danny and Sara
were hanging by their knees,
but Jim's hands
would not let go.

Upside down, he could see Willy and Sammy.
Sammy was showing Willy his ketchup
collection from Burg-o-land.
"Look how many I have!" he said.

Jim could see the new girl. Her name was
Elinor Woodman, from Chicago, Illinois.
She was shooting baskets.

Jim heard Anna Maria talking to Margaret
and George. "The most popular person
in first grade is Paul," she said.

"And you are the second
most popular, Margaret.
And I am the third."

Jim got off the jungle gym. He tried to think
how to be more popular.
What if he started a club?
"I am starting a club," he told everybody.

"Do you want to join?" he asked.

Everybody did, except Elinor Woodman.

"Now," Jim said, "when you see somebody
that's in the club, you shake your head.
Three shakes is H. One shake is E.
Two is L—you have to do that twice.
And no shakes is O. That spells 'HELLO.' "

"I'm getting dizzy," said George.
"Is that all we do in this club?
I'm quitting," Danny said.
"Me too!"

"Hey, wait!" Jim tried to stop them.
But they all ran away.

"They quit my club!" Jim said to Elinor Woodman.
"So what?" she said.

After recess, the nurse took the first grade
to her office to get measured.
Paul was 3 feet 11 inches.
Willy was 3 feet 10 inches.

Sammy was 3 feet 9¾ inches.

Danny was 3 feet 11½ inches.

Anna Maria was 3 feet 10 inches.

And Jim was 3 feet 9½ inches.

Danny shouted, "Yaaay! I'm 3 feet 11½ inches! I'm the tallest."

"You bragged," said Anna Maria and
she went to tell the teacher.

"I'm too short," Jim said.

But Sara said, "Sometimes it's good to be short."

"When is it? When?" asked Jim.

"Well, you don't have to bend over
  so much," Sara said.

And Elinor Woodman said,
"So Danny's 3 feet 11½ inches, and you're
3 feet 9½ inches. So what?"

After lunch there was gym. They were doing
square dancing. Jim loved it when they swung
their arms and shouted "Yah-hoo!"
He loved going in the "grand right and left."

He was dancing and dancing when the teacher touched his arm. "Kevin," she said, "try to listen to the music."

Kevin? Who is Kevin? Jim wondered.

"Oh, Jim, I'm sorry. I have a Kevin
in my other class and he can't keep
in step either," said the teacher.

Jim asked to go to the bathroom. When he
came out, Elinor Woodman was coming
from the girls' bathroom.
"What's the matter?" she asked.
"I can't do anything right," Jim said.

"Look," said Elinor Woodman.
"Some things are easy for some people
and hard for other people. So what?"

"So what! So what!" Jim said. "Maybe in Chicago, Illinois, they say, 'So what?' Here it's different!"

"OK," said Elinor Woodman.

Every day Jim hung upside down
and couldn't let go.
And every day Elinor
Woodman practiced
shooting baskets.

Then one day, he didn't see her.
"Elinor Woodman has gone back to
Chicago, Illinois," Anna Maria said, "and
we'll never see her again."

Jim went to think on the jungle gym.
He thought about not being the most
popular person in first grade.

He thought about his club that nobody
but him belonged to. He thought
about being 3 feet 9½ inches tall.

Suddenly he said, "So what?"
And his hands let go of the bar
and he was hanging by his knees.